This igloo book belongs to:

....

igloobooks

Written by Gemma Barder
Illustrated by Ela Jarzabek,
Robert Dunn, and Emma Foster

Cover designed by Nicholas Gage
Interiors designed by Katie Messenger
Edited by Natalia Boileau

Copyright © 2017 Igloo Books Ltd

An imprint of Bonnier Publishing USA
251 Park Avenue South, New York, New York 10010

Manufactured in China. HUN001 1117
10 9 8 7 6 5 4 3 2 1

Library of Congress Cataloging-in-Publication
Data is available upon request.

ISBN 978-1-4998-8038-0
IglooBooks.com
bonnierpublishingusa.com

My First
Treasury of
Animal
Stories

igloobooks

Contents

Gemma's Special Surprise

Gemma was the friendliest giraffe you could ever wish to meet.
She was always kind and polite, she gave everyone big giraffe smiles
each day, and, more than anything, she loved to help her friends.

Gemma would stretch up to the highest branch to reach the tastiest leaves for Zoe . . .

. . . she gave Lenny a ride on her back when he was too tired to walk . . .

. . . she even helped to untangle Emma's trunk.

Gemma's friends wanted to surprise her with an extra-special gift to say thank you for all her help, but they just didn't know what to get that would be special enough.

"I know!" said Zoe. "Let's make a pie from tasty leaves." But without Gemma's help, no one could reach the best leaves at the top of the tree.

9

Emma had another idea.
"How about we make her a beautiful flower bouquet?"
So, she gathered the prettiest flowers from all over the jungle.

But the flowers made Emma sneeze and with one mighty
"A-A-CHOO!"
the entire bouquet was blown away.

10

Just when the animals were about to give up hope of finding a special gift, Lenny jumped to his feet. **"I've got it!"** he said. **"Gemma helps us all the time. Maybe we should spend the day helping her?"**

The animals treated Gemma like she was the queen of the jungle.

Lenny brushed
her mane . . .

. . . Zoe polished her hooves . . .

. . . and Emma gave her a relaxing neck massage.

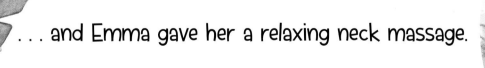

"**Helping is fun!**" said the animals. Gemma smiled.
"**And that's exactly why I love helping all of you,**" she said,
with a gigantic giraffe smile on her face.

Little Bunny's First Day

It was Little Bunny's first day at forest school and she was so excited that she hopped and skipped extra fast to get there on time. **"I'm going to be the best bunny in the whole school,"** she said, giggling as she hopped ahead of her mom.

But when Little Bunny arrived at the school gate, she felt a bit lost. There were lots of bigger bunnies, hopping around and playing with their friends, and Little Bunny didn't know anyone.

15

In class, Little Bunny listened eagerly as Miss Bounce asked the class lots of questions. Although Little Bunny knew the answers to some questions, there were lots of things she didn't know, too.

She shrank down in her seat, feeling sad.

The last lesson of the day was hopping class. Little Bunny started quickly and was determined to hop the highest and bounce the fastest, but she tripped over her own feet and landed flat on her bottom.

When Little Bunny got home from school, she slumped down in her bed and told her mom everything that had happened. **"Oh, Little Bunny,"** said her mom softly. **"You can't be the best straight away. You go to school to learn."**

The next day, Little Bunny knew exactly what to do.
In the morning, she scurried past the bigger bunnies . . .

. . . and made friends with a group of other young bunnies from her class.
Little Bunny realized that the playground wasn't so scary after all.

In class, Little Bunny put up her hand to ask Miss Bounce a question if she didn't know the answer.

Little Bunny still tripped over in hopping class, but she just giggled and jumped right back up again.

At the end of the week, Little Bunny was thrilled to be presented with a trophy for trying the hardest in class.

"I might not be the best at everything, but I'm the best at trying, and that's all that matters," Little Bunny said proudly.

Marina's Perfect Present

Deep in the ocean, Marina had spent all morning making a beautiful shell necklace for her mom. She was just about to thread on the last pretty shell when her brother, Finley, swam over to her.

"What's that?" asked Finley, giggling.
"I made a necklace for Mom," replied Marina proudly.

"You can't give that to her!" he said, laughing rudely.
"That's just a bunch of boring old shells on string."

Marina began to sob. **"He's right,"** she thought, tossing the necklace into some seaweed. **"I need to find something better to give Mom."**

Just then, Marina spotted something glistening on the seabed.

It was a bright shining pearl!
"Mom would love that,"
gasped Marina. But just as
she reached for the pearl . . .

... **SNAP!**

The clam slammed
shut and nipped
Marina's fin.

Marina was still determined
to find the perfect present.
As she swam over a coral
reef, she had a wonderful idea.

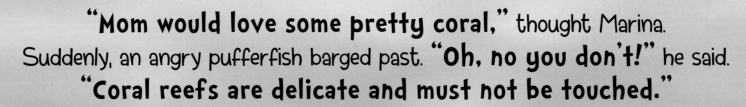

"**Mom would love some pretty coral**," thought Marina. Suddenly, an angry pufferfish barged past. "**Oh, no you don't!**" he said. "**Coral reefs are delicate and must not be touched.**"

"**I'm sorry!**" cried Marina, swimming away as fast as she could. Just then, she remembered one last place to look.

Marina searched an old shipwreck and suddenly she spotted a treasure chest full of glittering jewels. She was sure to find the perfect present for her mom.

But as she moved to get a closer look, a wriggly octopus wiggled over. **"Hands off!"** he said. **"This is my treasure."** Marina darted away as fast as she could.

Feeling sad, Marina swished her tail and swam home. **"Now I don't have anything to give Mom,"** she said.

Little did Marina know, her mom was following close behind.

To Marina's delight, her mom was wearing the seashell necklace. "I love it!" beamed Mom. "It was clever of you to hide it in the seaweed." "But it's just homemade," said Marina, looking surprised.

Marina's mom smiled. "That's exactly why it's so special."

The Flying Penguin

Penguins are great at lots of things, like catching fish
and swimming, but one thing they can't do at all is fly.

Unfortunately for Percy the penguin, his
biggest dream was to do just that.

Even though his penguin friends on Flipper Beach told him he'd
never be able to fly, Percy was determined to prove them wrong.

So, he climbed to the top of a nearby rock,
waddled to the edge, and took one big leap.

Thump! Poor Percy landed in a pile of soggy seaweed.
"Ouch!" he said grumpily.

But as Percy cleaned himself up, he had a great idea. **"I just need better wings,"** he said, gathering together as much seaweed as he could.

32

With his new seaweed wings,
Percy climbed to the top of an
even bigger rock than before.

He ran and ran,
and flipped and flapped.
Could he do it this time?

SPLOSH!

Percy landed in the sea
with a plop. It was hopeless!

Just then, a friendly pelican swooped down.
"If you want to fly, maybe I can help?" he said.
"Just hop into my beak and I'll take you up!"

Percy peered into the pelican's beak.
At long last, he was actually going to fly!

34

As he peeked out from the pelican's beak, Percy could see the frozen land beneath him growing smaller. **"Wow!"** he gasped, as the icy air rushed through his feathers.

Percy the penguin was really flying, and it felt . . .

35

. . . well, it felt a bit scary, actually. In the distance, Percy spotted his friends on Flipper Beach. They were so far below that they looked like little ants.

Percy could see for miles across the ocean and it looked frighteningly big. **"Erm, could you take me back down now, please?"** he asked the pelican.

Back on Flipper Beach, the pelican returned Percy to the safety of his huddle, then flew up, up, and away. Percy felt the ice beneath his feet and breathed a sigh of relief. **"Perhaps penguins shouldn't fly after all,"** he decided.

The Ele-monkey

There was once a little elephant named Ella who was all alone in the jungle, until she met a friendly family of monkeys.

"We'll look after her and teach her to be just like us," chattered the monkeys, excitedly.

Ella copied everything the monkeys did. She climbed trees and balanced on branches, but she liked eating nuts and bananas best of all.

"Being a monkey is so much fun!" she cried.

As Ella grew bigger, she couldn't do the things she used to anymore. When she balanced on branches they snapped . . .

. . . all of the water whooshed out from the water hole when she jumped in for a bath . . .

. . . and the little nuts were too complicated for her to open.

Ella wasn't as happy as she used to be. Her nose was longer, her ears were bigger, and she needed to eat ten times as many bananas than before!

"Why am I so different?" she sighed.

Suddenly, the ground shook and Ella saw someone who looked just like her. **"Hello,"** said a friendly elephant. **"Where's your herd?"**

"I don't have a herd," replied Ella, looking confused. **"I'm a monkey."**

"Don't be silly," said the friendly elephant, chuckling. **"You are an elephant!"**

42

The friendly elephant smiled and lifted his trunk. **"Did you know you could do this?"**

TRUUUUMPET!

"And how about this?" he said, spraying water out of his trunk. Ella hadn't realized she could do such fun things with her trunk.

The friendly elephant introduced Ella to his herd. For the first time in her life, she actually felt small.

Ella spent the day learning how to roll around and swoosh cooling mud on her back.

She even played stampede chase with the younger elephants in the herd.

It was soon time for Ella to live with the elephant herd. She felt sad to leave her monkey family, but the kind elephants told her they would look after her. The monkeys gave Ella a big monkey hug. **"You can visit us whenever you like,"** they said.

"You will always be a silly monkey to us."

Harry the Hero

Life wasn't easy for Harry the donkey. He lived with four beautiful horses who had long legs and shiny coats. While the horses were sleek and fast, Harry was shaggy and slow. **"I wish I was special,"** he sighed sadly.

The tallest and fastest of all
the horses was Lightning.
He spent his days galloping and
prancing around in the paddock.

Lightning's favorite thing
of all was to show just how
fast he could run and
how high he could jump.

47

The other horses soon had enough of Lightning showing off, so they trotted to the other side of the paddock for some peace. **"Watch this!"** boasted Lightning to Harry, as he galloped towards a high haystack at the edge of the field.

Lightning leaped over the haystack as Harry looked
on in amazement, when suddenly . . .

... SPLAT!

Lightning landed in a deep patch of wet, gloopy mud. **"I'm stuck!"**
cried Lightning, looking very worried. **"Help me, Harry!"**

"How can I help?" asked Harry in a panic. "I'm far too small." Just then, he realized there was one thing he could do better than anyone. He took a deep breath and . . .

"HEE HAW!"

"HEE HAW!"

Harry called and called, until, finally, the other horses galloped across the field. **"Lightning is stuck!"** said Harry, out of breath. **"Fetch some rope, quickly."** The horses did exactly what Harry said.

Lightning held on to one end of the rope with his teeth, while all the other horses pulled on the other end. **"It's no use,"** said Lightning hopelessly.

"Harry, you need to help, too!" cried Lightning.
Harry gulped and took hold of the rope.

With one last heave, the horses and Harry pulled Lightning free. **"Thank you,"** Lightning said gratefully. **"We couldn't have done it without you, Harry,"** the other horses added. Harry smiled. He felt just as special as everyone else.

53

The Island Parade

The island parade was the most exciting, most fun day of the year. Everyone made sure they looked their best as they danced and pranced through the jungle and along the beach.

But Tom the giant tortoise wasn't looking forward to the parade at all. He looked at his friends and sighed. Patti the parrot was bright and beautiful, Max the monkey was athletic and strong, and as for Tim and Ted the tigers? Their fur was magnificent.

"My shell used to be so bright and shiny.
Now it's old and dull," said Tom unhappily.

"I'm not taking part in the parade looking like this," he added
with a sigh, then he skulked back to his home by the water hole to sleep.

"It won't be the same without Tom," sighed Max. "He's been in the parade longer than anyone." Just then, Patti flapped her bright wings excitedly. "I've got it!" she said. "I know exactly how we can help."

Patti told them to collect anything bright they could find.
Together, they collected . . .

. . . beautiful flowers . . .   . . . colorful feathers . . .

. . . and shimmering shells.

The next day, Tom woke up feeling miserable. It was the morning of the parade, and for the first time ever, he wasn't going to take part.

He was just about to take a slurp at the water hole, when he noticed the most amazing, colorful reflection staring back at him. **"Is that really me?"** he gasped.

As the parade was about to start, Max, Patti, Tim, and Ted searched for Tom. **"Maybe he didn't like the surprise?"** said Patti.

Max climbed to the top of the tallest tree. **"I can see him!"** he cried excitedly.

Everyone cheered as Tom proudly strode past, decorated
with the feathers, flowers, and shells his friends had collected.
He was the most colorful tortoise, ever!

The Big Bad Mouse

One day, Smudge the kitten came to live in a new house, but the house was already home to a big, grumpy, ginger cat named Jasper. **"What do we have here?"** said Jasper, jabbing Smudge with his paw.

"**I'm Smudge,**" replied the kitten timidly. Jasper looked at Smudge menacingly. He'd never seen such a little kitten before. "**I might be tiny,**" said Smudge, shaking, "**but I'm just as tough as you!**"

63

Just then, a little mouse scurried across the kitchen floor looking for tasty scraps. Smudge squealed and hid behind Jasper's legs.

"It's just a mouse!" said Jasper, bursting into laughter, as he rolled around on the floor.

64

"Whoever heard of a cat afraid of a mouse?"

said Jasper, then he went off to nap in the sunshine.

Smudge sighed and flopped on to the floor. Just then,
a small, twitchy nose poked out from the skirting board.

Smudge began to tremble as the mouse tiptoed closer. **"I'm Titch. You don't need to be afraid of me,"** squeaked the little mouse. **"I won't hurt you."** Smudge smiled and soon the cat and the mouse were friends.

"Jasper always chases me around the house," sighed poor Titch miserably. "If only there was a way to teach him a lesson."

Just then, Smudge came up with a fantastic idea.

That night, Titch hid behind
the sofa with a pan, a wooden spoon,
and two large paper plates.

As Jasper was settling down
to sleep for the night, Titch
banged and clanged the spoon on
the pan as hard as he could.

Jasper jumped into the air, his fur standing on end. As he looked up, he saw a pair of giant mouse ears peeking out from behind the sofa.

"It's a monster mouse!" wailed Jasper, trembling from nose to tail.

69

Suddenly, Smudge ran into the living room. **"I'll save you, Jasper!"** he cried bravely, as he leapt behind the sofa. Jasper watched in amazement as the mouse ears disappeared and the loud noises stopped. **"Smudge is a hero!"** gasped Jasper.

70

Smudge reappeared without a whisker out of place. **"I'm sorry for being so mean,"** said Jasper. That night, Jasper let Smudge sleep right next to him on the softest sofa cushion, and he never chased Titch again.

No Swimming for Stanley

Stanley loved almost everything about being a polar bear. He loved rolling down hills, chasing his brothers and sisters, and he even loved the snow. But there was just one small thing that Stanley didn't like: swimming.

Whenever Stanley got too close to the water's edge, he would scamper back in the snow and hide between his mom's legs. **"It's far too deep,"** Stanley whimpered. **"And much too cold. What if I freeze?"**

Stanley's friends decided to help. Sally the seal showed him how fun it was to dive in and out of the water.

But Stanley shook his head.
"I'd never be able to do that," he said sadly.

Scully the seagull showed Stanley how easy it was to catch delicious fish by darting into the waves.

But Stanley just covered his eyes. **"I'm far too slow to catch slippery fish,"** he sighed.

Finally, Fred the arctic fox cub decided to teach Stanley how to be brave. **"Close your eyes and imagine you're as big as a mountain,"** he said.

Stanley closed his eyes and took a deep breath, when suddenly, he heard a loud splash.

Fred had slipped and fallen in the icy water, but he was
only a little cub and hadn't learned how to swim properly.

"Somebody help me!" cried Fred. Stanley looked around, but there
wasn't anyone else who could help. There was only one thing to do . . .

... **Splosh!** Stanley jumped into the water and paddled as fast as he could.

Fred jumped on Stanley's back and together they climbed back on to the snowy bank. **"You did it. You swam!"** gasped Fred, beaming proudly.

Soon, Stanley was swimming every day. The water became less scary and it wasn't too cold thanks to his thick, snuggly fur. He played with Sally, caught fish with Scully, and always gave Fred a ride on his back.

Pepper to the Rescue

Pepper the puppy wanted to be just like his Uncle Rover,
a famous tracking dog who lived in the deepest jungles.

Although Pepper practiced
tracking every day, he could
never imagine being as
good as Rover.

One afternoon, while Pepper was tracking the scent of a scurrying squirrel, his mom told him some very exciting news.

"Rover is coming to stay," she said. Pepper jumped for joy.
"I'll have to practice my tracking skills twice as hard now!"

The day of Rover's visit finally arrived. Pepper watched eagerly as Rover showed him his impressive compass collar. **"The most important thing a good tracking dog needs,"** said Rover, **"is his nose."**

"A-A-CHOO!"

Suddenly, Rover let out a big sneeze.

That afternoon, Pepper and Rover roamed through the forest, splashed through puddles, and dug in the undergrowth. But poor Rover kept sneezing.

"Are you sick?" asked Pepper, looking concerned.
"Of course not!" replied his uncle. "Us tracking dogs don't get sick."

The next morning, Pepper bounded downstairs for
more fun with Rover, but he was nowhere to be seen.

"Rover went tracking early this morning,"
said Pepper's mom. "He's been gone quite some time."

Pepper decided to look for Rover using the tracking skills his uncle had taught him. In the backyard, Pepper found Rover's lost compass in the grass.

Next, Pepper sniffed and sniffed and soon discovered a scent trail.

Following his nose, he found a trail of paw prints, too!

The paw prints led Pepper to the forest.
Suddenly, he spotted Rover looking very lost.

"Thank goodness, Pepper!"
said Rover. "I think I might have
a cold after all. I lost my compass
and couldn't sniff my way home."

Back home, Rover gave Pepper his very own compass. **"It's used by the best tracker dogs and after today, that includes you,"** he said proudly. Pepper gave Rover a big hug. **"I have the best teacher, ever,"** he said, smiling.

The Loudest Lion

Leo was the smallest cub in the pride. While his brother and sister played together, Leo just sat alone. **"You're too small to play with us,"** his siblings would say. One day, Leo was so fed up of being ignored that he let out a long, loud . . .

. . .ROAR!

Leo's mom came bounding towards him. **"Are you okay?"** she asked, looking worried. **"Your roar is very special. You must only use it when you really need to."** Leo admitted there was nothing wrong.

The next day, Leo was trying to get a drink at the water hole, but the bigger animals kept pushing him out of the way. Leo knew just what to do. He took a big, deep breath and . . .

The hippos hopped . . .

. . . the giraffe jumped . . .

. . . and the elephant trumpeted!

Soon, the water hole was empty.
Leo giggled and took a nice long drink.
He felt very pleased with himself.

Leo decided that roaring was far too much fun to leave for a special occasion. So he roared at lunchtime to get the most food, and roared in the afternoon while everyone was trying to nap.

Leo headed into the jungle to look for more mischief,
but soon he found himself in trouble.

A thick vine had tangled around his paw. No matter
how hard he tried, Leo just couldn't free himself.
"I know!" he thought, **"I'll just roar for help."**

Leo roared with all his might,
but no one came to help him.
All the other animals just thought
it was Leo being silly again.

ROAR

As night began to fall, Leo tried
one last roar, but he'd roared so
much that he lost his voice.

Leo was feeling very sorry for himself. Before long, his mom appeared and freed him from the vine. **"I couldn't find you anywhere. I've been so worried,"** she said, looking concerned.

"I roared and roared but no one came to save me. They all thought I was just pretending," squeaked Leo. **"And now I've lost my roar. Will it ever come back?"**

Leo's mom hugged him close and smiled.
"Your roar will be as good as new in the morning," she said.

"And from now on, you'll know exactly the right way to use it."